Bluey

BOB BILBY

PENGUIN YOUNG READERS LICENSES
An Imprint of Penguin Random House LLC, New York

This book is based on the TV series *Bluey*.

First published in Australia in 2020 by Puffin Books. Published in the United States in 2021 by Penguin Young Readers Licenses, an imprint of Penguin Random House LLC, New York. Manufactured in China.

Visit us online at www.penguinrandomhouse.com.

ISBN 9780593224595   10 9 8 7 6 5 4

Hi, my name is Bob. I'm a bilby. I like making new **FRIENDS** and having **FUN TIMES** with them. Like most bilbies, I'm not much of a talker.

Today I'm going home with Bingo Heeler. She seems really nice. I'm already **FRIENDS** with her sister, Bluey.

I wonder what we'll get up to.

At Bingo's house, I show her family my book. It has photos of all the adventures I've had with my **FRIENDS**.

This is Jasper W.
He likes Australian rules
football.

This is me on a trip
with Mrs. Terrier. It was
cold in Scotland.

Look at my yellow
karate belt here!

Every new **FRIEND** has
their own way to have
FUN TIMES.

5

"Oh, you did a bit of karate, Bob," says Bingo's mum. "Wackadoo!"

I sure did! I learned it when I stayed with my **FRIEND** Maxie.

HEE-YA!

Bingo's ready to show me how she has **FUN TIMES**.
But first, that sausage roll the big blue guy has looks yum.

We play Moo Cow, and Bluey and Bingo show me the tablet. I've never seen one before. It can take photos.

CLICK!

moo!

9

You can also play games on it.

Bingo's mum and dad have tablets, too.
I wonder if they play games as well.

CLICK!

We watch cartoons on the way to the shops. I love watching cartoons. The cartoon characters have so much fun.

"Don't you want to teach Bob some car games?"
asks Bingo's mum.

Maybe after the cartoons are finished.

At the shops, we watch even more cartoons on an even bigger tablet! So many pretty colors.

Bingo's mum watches hockey on the big tablets, too.
I love hockey. I wonder if Bingo and I will play hockey
when we get home.

We don't. We watch more cartoons. I think I'm ready to do something else with Bingo now. Our time together is almost over.

"Kids, I'm putting our photos in Bob Bilby's book," calls Bingo's mum. She's been taking photos all day.

But when Bingo looks at the book, she sees the photos are all just of me watching cartoons. Bingo gets upset.

Bluey seems to understand. "Bob just copies everything we do, and all we're doing is really **BORING** stuff. So we need to do some really **EXCITING** stuff instead!"

She takes all their tablets and puts them in a basket.

Bingo's mum gets out the bikes.
Bingo and I are about to have **FUN TIMES**!

The big blue guy takes
photos of our adventures.

We play at the park and get dizzy going round and round.

We ride on Sparklemane and pretend she can fly.

The fireworks are my favorite thing ever.
So many pretty colors.
I love my **FRIEND** Bingo.

20

Back at kindergarten, Bingo and I tell the class about our **FUN TIMES** together and show them the new photos in my book.

Then it's time for me to have an adventure with Missy.
I'm going to miss Bingo.

I hope she knows how happy I am that we're **FRIENDS**.

She seems upset again.

I want to tell Bingo that I had so much fun with her, and I can't wait to see her again.

23

But I'm not much of a talker.